July 14, 2007
Your 1st Trip to the Zoo
Brevard Zoo, Viera Florida
Love,
Mima, Beepa, Daddy + Mommy
We love you!

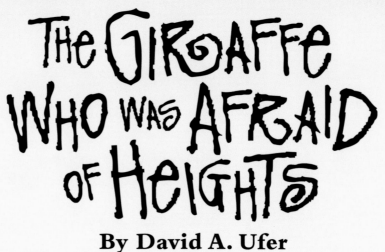

The Giraffe Who Was Afraid of Heights

By David A. Ufer
Illustrated by Kirsten Carlson

The author donates a portion of his royalties from this book to the World Wildlife Fund.
Thanks to educators at the Houston Zoo for verifying the accuracy of the "For Creative Minds" section.

For BillieJo—thank you for all that you do and all that you mean to me.
And for Ms. Virginia Castleman—thank you for your support and guidance and all your encouraging words. – DAU
To everyone who chooses to face their fear, and not run away...even when it has big, scary teeth. – KC

Library of Congress Control Number: 2005931002
ISBN 13: 978-0-9768823-0-5
ISBN 10: 0-9768823-0-2
Text Copyright © David A. Ufer 2006
Illustration Copyright © Kirsten Carlson 2006
Creative Minds Copyrights © Sylvan Dell Publishing 2006
Text Layout and Design by Lisa Downey
Printed in China
Sylvan Dell Publishing
976 Houston Northcutt Blvd., Suite 3
Mt. Pleasant, SC 29464

www.SylvanDellPublishing.com
Copyright@SylvanDellPublishing.com

ONCE upon a time on the African savannah there lived a family of beautiful giraffes. There was a father, a mother, and a young son. The parents were very proud of their son.

THERE was only one problem with their son—he was afraid of heights. He could not lift his head above his shoulders without getting scared and falling. His parents always had to watch for lions that could hurt him because he could not see above the grass himself. They decided to send him to the village doctor for help.

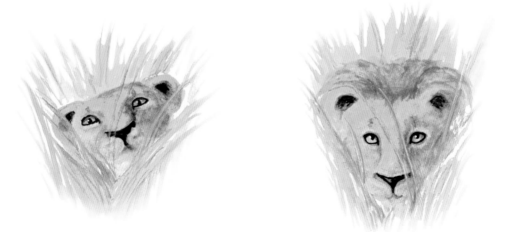

The parents gave the young giraffe a map to the doctor's office and sent him on his way. The path twisted and turned as it followed a river. The young giraffe smelled the plants that lined the path.

he rounded a bend in the path, the giraffe saw a young monkey sitting on the ground drawing pictures in the dirt.

"Hello," the giraffe said to the monkey.

"Hi," she replied.

"Nice to meet you," said the giraffe. "What are you doing?"

"I AM supposed to go to the doctor today because I'm afraid of climbing trees. I'm in danger of getting hurt by other animals on the ground. The doctor is going to help me."

"Wow!" cried the giraffe. "I'm going to the doctor, too. I'm afraid of heights. We can go together."

"Let's go," answered the monkey.

The two new friends walked down the path until they came to a spot where the path crossed the river. A young hippo sat and cried in the grass at the edge of the river.

"What's wrong?" asked the giraffe.

"**WELL,** I need to go to the doctor today because I'm afraid of the water; but I'm too scared to cross the river," sobbed the hippo.

"Guess what! We're on our way to the village to see the doctor, too. Maybe we can find a way for you to go with us," said the giraffe.

"I don't see how. I can't get across the river."

THE giraffe and hippo sat by the path trying to come up with an answer to their problem while the monkey dangled her feet in the river and gently kicked the water.

BUT the kicking of her feet attracted the attention of a crocodile. It slowly made its way through the water. As it approached the monkey, it raised its head out of the water and opened its mouth very wide—ready to eat lunch!

"help, there's a crocodile after me!" the monkey cried as she ran away from the river.

"Come here, quick! Jump onto my head!" shouted the giraffe.

The monkey leapt onto the giraffe's head and he lifted her as high as possible. The giraffe's long legs shook, sending a chill clear up his long, stiff, scared self. The shiver didn't stop until it reached his head. Or maybe the shaking was the monkey, who trembled as she held his ears.

THE monkey jumped into one of the trees, grabbed some coconuts, and threw them at the crocodile.

 then the hippo charged the crocodile. The crocodile ran away as fast as he could, but the hippo chased after him at full speed! They both crashed into the river, sending a huge spray of water into the air. The two fought, turning each other over and over until the crocodile decided he had had enough and swam away.

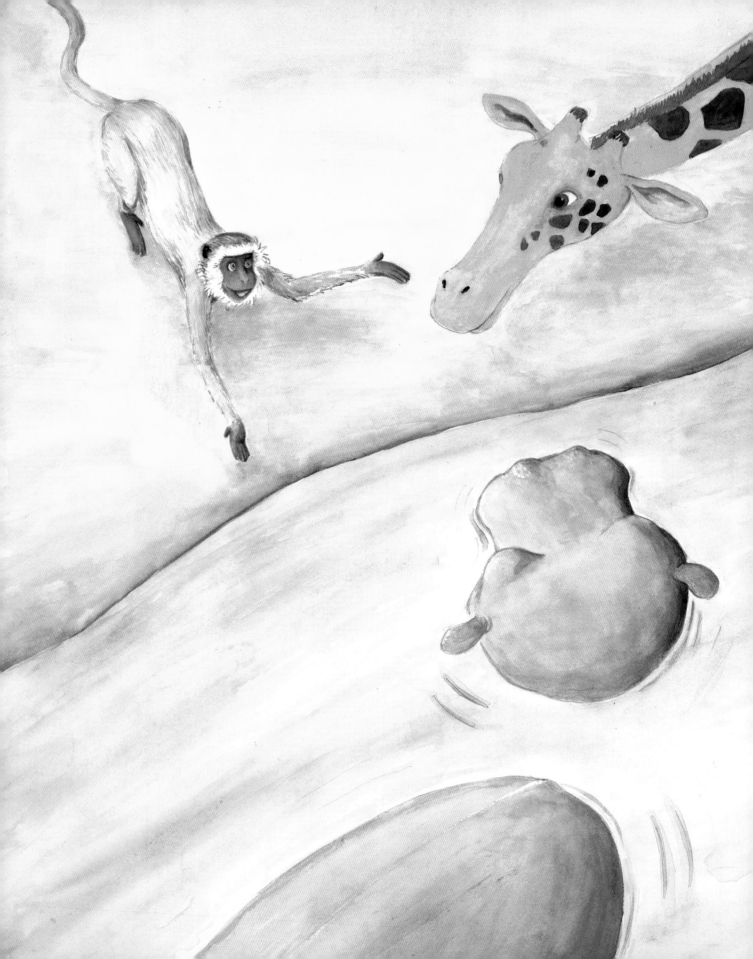

"YOU stay away from my friends!" roared the hippo as he watched the crocodile swim away.

"Hey, you were awesome. You saved my life," the monkey said to the hippo. "You jumped into that river and chased that crocodile away!"

She turned to the giraffe, "And you lifted me into the tree so I wouldn't get eaten!"

**"Hey,** do you know what that means?" asked the giraffe.

"We aren't afraid anymore! We don't have to go to the doctor!" The hippo played and swam in the river. The monkey collected coconuts from high in the trees. The giraffe proudly held his head in the air, watching for hungry predators.

For Creative Minds

Is it Fact or Fiction?

Animals don't really play and talk to each other the way they do in this story. That means that this is a make-believe story. There wouldn't really be coconut trees in the African Savannah (but they would be in the African rainforest or jungle). A baby hippo would probably not really be able to scare off an adult crocodile; but an adult hippo could. What *is* true is that all animals have different behaviors or adaptations that help them survive where they live and to get their food and water.

Animal Adaptations

Giraffes

The giraffes' long necks and legs are adaptations that help them reach high into trees to eat the leaves. Because their necks are so long, giraffes can reach leaves that are higher than any other animal can reach to eat.

Because giraffes are so tall, they can also see all around and often see predators while they are a long way away. That gives them time to run away.

The giraffes' long tongues let them easily break the leaves off the tree.

The spots of different sizes and colors help them to blend into their surrounding area and to camouflage themselves.

Giraffes have hoofed feet that are good for standing and running on rough and uneven land.

Vervet Monkeys

Vervet monkeys spend most of their time living in or around trees. They climb high into the trees to sleep or when they are scared.

Monkeys' eyes are located close together and in the front of their heads, just like ours. This helps the monkeys to judge distances so they can jump from one branch to another.

A vervet's long tail helps it to keep its balance as it moves through the trees.

Monkeys have hands similar to ours—they even have fingernails! Some monkeys, like the vervet monkeys, have "thumbs" that help them grab and hold onto things. Humans have the same "thumb" adaptation. *To see what life would be like without your thumbs, tape your thumbs down and see how long you can go without using them! What can't you do without your thumbs?*

Monkeys even have toes on their feet.

Common Hippopotamus or Hippo

The hippos' eyes, noses, and ears are on the top of their heads so they can see, breathe, and hear while they lay low in the water.

They close their nostrils (noses) and fold down their ears when they go under water.

Hippos' feet have four toes and small webs between the toes to help them "walk" underwater.

Nile Crocodile

Just like the hippo, crocodiles have their eyes & noses high on their heads so they can see and breathe while "hiding" underwater. When "hiding," they look just like logs floating in the water.

And, just like the hippo, crocodiles can close their noses and ears when they go underwater. Unlike the hippo, crocodiles have "see-through" eyelids so they can see underwater.

The strong claw feet are used to grab prey and hold it underwater. The claws help crocodiles to crawl up onto land, to dig holes for water, and to help the females to dig nests in which to lay their eggs.

Crocodiles use sharp teeth to tear apart their food.

Fun Facts

Giraffes

- Giraffes have only 7 bones (vertebrae) in their long necks—the same as we have! Their bones or vertebrae are just much longer than ours.

- Their necks are so long that they must spread their front legs to be able to drink.

- Adult giraffes' tongues are over 18 inches long. *Measure 18 inches to see how long their tongues are!*

- A baby giraffe is about 6 feet tall when it is born. *How tall are you? How tall are your mother, father, and teacher? Who is tallest? How long were you when you were born?*

- On average a fully-grown giraffe is about 16 feet tall. The male is about two feet taller than the female. *Measure 16 feet.*

Vervet Monkey or Green Monkey

- Just like there are many different types of cats and dogs, there are many different types of monkeys. The monkey in this story is a vervet monkey that lives in Africa and some parts of the Caribbean. *Can you find those places on a map?* The vervets in the Caribbean are probably descendants of monkeys that were brought over on ships as pets by the early European explorers and settlers.

- Snakes, eagles, leopards, and crocodiles are their predators. If a vervet monkey sees trouble, it calls out an alarm to the others. There are special calls to "say" snake, eagle, or leopard!

- They are awake and active during the day and sleep at night.

- Fully-grown monkeys are between 18 and 26 inches tall and weigh between 7 and 17 pounds.

Common Hippopotamus or Hippo

- The word "Hippopotamus" actually means "river horse" in Greek because they spend most of their day in the water—playing or sleeping. They crawl out of the river to look for food at night.

- Hippos only eat grass and plants (herbivores).

- Baby hippos are born on land or in the water. They can nurse underwater.

- A hippo weighs around 100 pounds when it is born. *How much did you weigh when you were born? What do you weigh now? Who weighs more: you or a baby hippo?*

- Adult hippos may be about ten feet long and about four feet tall.

Nile Crocodile

- Crocodiles are egg-laying reptiles. The female sits on the nest of eggs until they are ready to hatch.

- A baby crocodile is about 12 inches long when it hatches.

- Adult crocodiles may be up to 16 feet long!

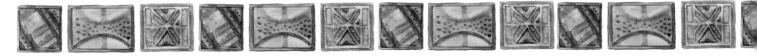

Matching Game

Using what you know about each animal, try to match the footprint to the correct animal.

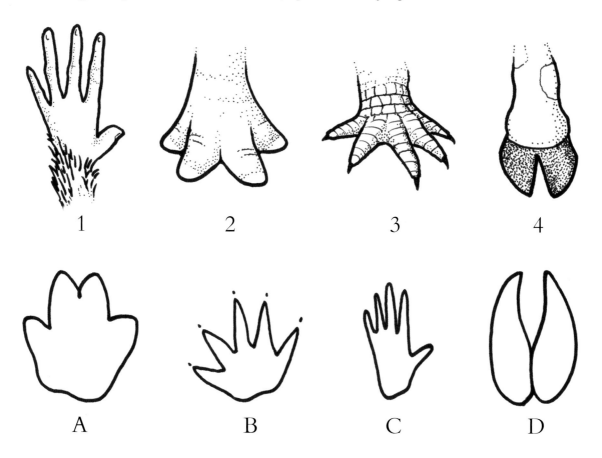

1   2   3   4

A   B   C   D

Craft Activity: Mix-and-Match Activity Book

On the next page you will find a template for a mix-and-match book. Here is how to make your book:

Photocopy or download the page.
Cut out each rectangle containing an animal.
Cut along the dotted line just up to the solid gray line (spine).
Staple the pages together along the spine.
Now you can color and mix and match your animals!

For easy use, the "For Creative Minds" section may be photocopied or downloaded from the ***The Giraffe Who was Afraid of Heights'*** book homepage at www.SylvanDellPublishing.com.

Matching Game answers: 1-C: monkey; 2-A: hippo; 3-B: crocodile; 4-D: giraffe

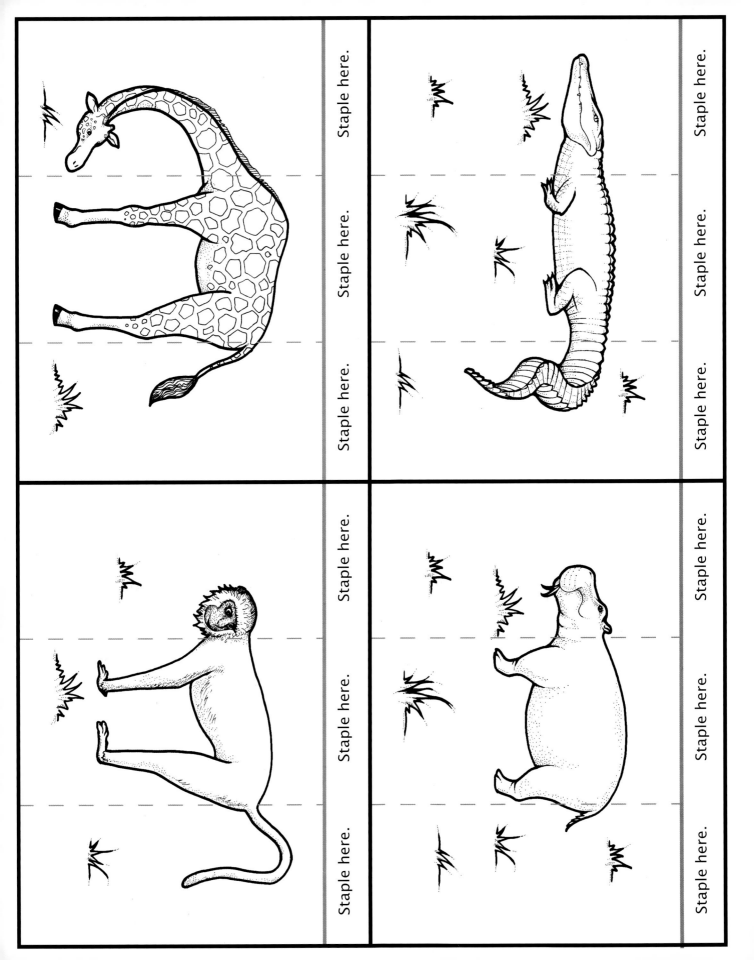

Staple here.

Staple here.

Staple here.

Staple here.

Staple here.

Staple here.

Staple here.

Staple here.

Staple here.

Staple here.

Staple here.

Staple here.